Caleb Johnson

Mountain Man

Menace in the Mountain Mist

Book Two

Charles Ray

D1534248

D.W.D.

1.

Much to his surprise, Caleb Johnson was finding that being hitched wasn't nearly as strange or unsettling as he'd expected it to be. In fact, he was finding it really quite pleasurable.

Every since he'd returned to his little cabin near Bear Creek, Colorado with Spring Flower, a Shoshone widow with him he'd developed a mutual attraction that turned to love during a winter-over with her village during his journey from Oregon, where he'd spent two years helping his unlikely best friend, former Confederate cavalry officer, Ben Winthrop get his horse ranch up and running, he'd found many things about marriage that were to his liking.

He no long had to cook all his own meals, or wash his clothes, or clean the cabin. He no longer had to spend the long, cold winter nights huddled under his blanket alone, or with Dog, his old hound who was now getting old and preferred sleeping by the iron stove.

Yep, he thought as he honed the blade of his knife, Ben was right. Married life ain't half bad.

Spring Flower, who was learning to read English, and was almost as good at reading as he was, had adopted the name, Flora, which he also found quite nice. One of the books she read diligently was the tattered dictionary he used frequently. In it, she'd discovered that flora meant flower, and decided that it would be better of folks around Bear Creek had a white name to call her by, because too many of them snickered every time they called her Spring Flower. Caleb allowed as how he had no objection to it, and thought it sounded as pretty as she looked, and from that day on, she was known as Mrs. Flora Johnson to all and sundry.

She was also mastering the art of cooking what she called white man's food. The griddle cakes, which, except for the sugar and cinnamon Caleb liked in them, weren' t all that different from the flat cakes made from ground corn that her people liked. Biscuits had been new to her, but once he'd shown her how to mix in the lard and milk just right so they baked up nice and fluffy, she found that she not only liked cooking them, but that with a little sugar syrup in or on them, they were really quite tasty.

Eggs had been a novelty to her, too. The Shoshone didn't raise chickens, and only on rare occasions would find and eat the eggs of wild birds, usually after putting them in hot ashes under the cooking fire, or boiling them in water. Scrambled eggs, with onion, pepper, and cheese fascinated her.

She had also made his cabin look like it had never looked before.

Elvira Stanhope, owner of a dress and dry goods shop that she operated next to her husband Tom's hardware store, had taken her under her wing and, in addition to making her several dresses to wear when she came to town, and for working around the cabin, had helped her pick out material which she showed her how to make into tablecloths and curtains. The place had never looked so bright, and after the first shock of seeing the blue and white tablecloth and matching curtains, Caleb found that he liked it, he liked it a lot.

He smiled warmly at her as she came out of the cabin's front door, a white apron over her usual nankeen britches and blue and white checked shirt. She smiled back.

"Caleb, it is time for lunch," she said.

"Be there directly." He put the knife back in its leather sheath and stood. "What are we havin' today?"

"I made the potato soup the way that Elizabeth taught me," she said. "And some biscuits to go with it."

He didn't remember eating biscuits with soup before, but it sounded good. He got up and walked to the water trough near the small barn, where he washed his hands and face. She had been adamant about him washing up before coming into the cabin, and before meals.

She was waiting for him when he entered the cabin. A large bowl containing a creamy substance was on the table at his customary place at the head. Next to it was a small plate with two biscuits, thick and golden brown, and a cup of coffee from which white vapors wafted. She sat to his right.

"That sure smells good," he said.

"I hope that it also tastes good."

"Shoot, Spri-, uh, Flora, everything you cook taste good. You're just about the best cook in Bear Creek."

She smiled shyly and lifted a spoon full of the creamy broth to her mouth. He paused, watching as she swallowed and nodded.

"I think it needs some more salt," she said.

He spooned some into his mouth. It was potato soup, with a hint of sage, and completely without lumps. She must have spent hours mashing the spuds, he thought.

"It's okay," he said. "A little salt wouldn't hurt, I s'pose."

She handed him the salt container.

"Please do not use too much, though," she said. "It will spoil the flavor of the sage."

He took a pinch, put it in, and stirred it. Then, he ate another spoonful.

"Hm, perfect. Jest the way I like it."

"You always say that. I know I am still learning to cook the white man's food."

The thing he liked about her, along with her great beauty, her cooking skills, and her devotion to him, was her modesty. Unlike many women he'd encountered, including Ben's wife Wenona, who could not resist occasionally bragging about how well she cooked, his Flora never boasted about the things she knew how to do; she just did them.

He smiled and patter her hand.

"You know, I need to go huntin' to store up some meat for the winter," he said.

She frowned at him.

"I know. Will you be gone long?"

"No, *we* won't be gone long. Maybe a week, ten days."

"We?" Her frown turned into an expression of confusion. "You wish for me to go with you?"

"Sure do. You can gather some of them herbs and plats you like," he said.

"That would be a good idea. When do we leave?"

"Well, I figure it'll take you a day or two to pack what you need. Today's Saturday, right? What say we leave Monday morning?"

She nodded and smiled.

"That would be fine. I will begin packing as soon as we finish our meal."

2.

Caleb wasn't planning on going too far, nor would he stay out too long. He figured three to five days would be enough time to bag enough game to provide them with meat through the winter, and for Flora to gather the herbs and plants she used to season food and treat winter ills.

After they finished eating, while Flora began laying out the clothing and other items from inside the house that she thought they would need on the trip, Caleb went out to the barn and began assembling the tools and equipment he'd need, which wasn't really all that much. He would be taking the pack horse, of course, to carry back any game he brought down, both of his rifles, spare ammunition, and a tent. If he'd been going out alone, he would've left the tent and made do with makeshift shelter, but he wouldn't have his wife sleeping any rougher than necessary. Besides, he thought, he was kind of looking forward to snuggling in a tent at night with her.

He tossed a few other odds and ends, like a short-handle shovel, a hatchet, and a pickaxe, onto the unfolded canvas tent, before folding it to strap across the pack horse's back for the trip out.

Satisfied that he had what he needed from the barn, he went back to the house, where he found that Flora had completed her packing. A neat bundle, tied with cord, sat on the kitchen table. To his surprise and delight, her bundle was less than half the size of his, so it would be no problem to include it his own. When he told her this, she insisted that her own pack horse could handle it, reminding him that his livestock had increased two-fold when they married, her bringing two horses of her own.

"This is gon' be quite the procession," he said. "Four horses 'n a dog. Hope we don' scare off all the game 'fore I get a chance to bag one or two young bucks."

She sniffed at him.

"My animals are well-behaved, husband. I do not, however, know about yours."

"Horse 'n Dog know how to act when I'm huntin'," he said, affecting to be offended by her remark, and failing, which caused her to giggle. "Now, I ain't so sure 'bout that pack horse my friend Ben give me. Guess we just have to wait 'n see."

"Are you sure you do not want to start our journey tomorrow, Caleb?"

He shook his head.

"Naw. Tomorrow's Sunday. I ain't exactly a religious man, but I always tries to treat Sunday as a day of rest. Gives me time to think about things."

She lifted the bundle from the table and placed it in the corner of the room.

"In that case, I will start cooking. This work has made me hungry."

He put both hands on her shoulders and pulled her back until her small frame nestled against his.

"I'm kinda hungry, too," he said. "But not for the kinda stuff that comes off the stove."

3.

They spent a quiet Sunday, sitting on chairs in front of the cabin, getting up only to refill their coffee cups, or to eat, comfortable in each other's company, without need of words, satisfied to enjoy their surroundings in silence. Dog seemed to sense their desire for silence. He lay at their feet, his muzzle resting on his crossed front legs, his only movement an occasional flicker of his tail, his only sound an occasional loud fart that thankfully was blown away from them by a gentle breeze that continued to waft over them.

That evening, they went to bed early, and rose with the sun the following day. Caleb took their bundles out to put on their pack horses, while Flora prepared a quick breakfast. After eating, they cleaned together, called Dog who had gone off into the trees to do his business, locked the cabin, mounted, and headed northwest into the foothills where they knew the herbs Flora sought grew, and where deer herds should be numerous.

The foothills were shrouded in the early morning mist that was common at this time of year, while the snow-capped peaks jutted through the mist and low-hanging clouds like giant sharks' teeth, clearly defined against the bright blue sky.

By midday, they had halved the distance between the cabin and the foothills, and stopped to eat. Caleb gathered wood and built a fire, while Flora set up a tripod of tree branches from which she suspended a kettle and the coffee pot. By the time the fire was going well, the aroma of beans and coffee filled the air. Flora put some strips of pork in an iron skillet and fried them until they were crisp and brown. She then made small patties of corn meal mixed with flakes of green pepper, salt, and water, and fried them in the pork grease.

"I think it'll be close to nightfall by the time we get to the foothills," Caleb said, as she spooned beans into his plate. "We'll camp at the base of the hills, 'n head up in the mornin'.'"

Flora glanced at the foothills, where the fog was beginning to disperse.

"I think it will be good for hunting," she said. "But it will be hard to find the plants I need in the early morning because of the mist."

"Ain't gon' be easy huntin' neither." Caleb spooned beans into his mouth, chewed a few times and swallowed. "Can't shoot what you can't see."

As she put pork and the fried bread on his plate, and began filling her own plate, she smiled at him, a smile he recognized as one of seduction.

"It will be nice to stay inside the tent until the mist is gone," she said.

Dog, who had been sitting quietly near the fire, watching her cook, moved to her side, and put his snout on her thigh. Caleb chuckled.

"I think Dog's askin' where his food is."

Smiling, Flora patted the animal's head, and picked up the dented metal bowl she'd set aside for him. She put beans and pork in the bowl, and put it on the ground near her feet. Dog plunged his snout in and began wolfing the food down like a starving man.

"Take your time, Dog," she said. "That is all you will get this time."

Dog stopped eating and looked up at her.

"I mean it," she said. "You will *not* get any of my food."

After swiping his tongue across his muzzle, Dog resumed eating.

"I don' think he b'lieves you," said Caleb.

"He knows me too well. Would you like me to pour you a cup of coffee?"

Caleb took the pot off the fire.

"Naw, I'll pour." He filled two cups, and handed one to her.

She took the cup and blew on it before taking a sip. Forgoing blowing on his coffee, Caleb put the cup to his lips.

"Ow! That's hot," he said.

She laughed softly.

"You are as bad as Dog, always rushing to eat or drink. You must learn to take your time, husband."

His cheeks turning red, and not just from the scalding coffee, Caleb smiled and nodded at her.

"As usual, wife, you're right. So, finish your food 'n drink your coffee. I'd like to get to the base of the hills 'fore it gets dark, so we can set up a proper camp."

She took another sip of coffee, looked down at Dog who had finished his food and was now eying her's with his tongue hanging out, and then scraped the remnants of her food into his bowl.

She made a sniffing sound.

"I do not know which is worse, the man or the dog." She smiled as she spoke.

Caleb returned the smile, but Dog ignored her and began gulping down the food.

She shook her head, waggled a finger at him, and began cleaning and storing the cooking utensils.

Having learned to work together on the trail on their journey from her village to Bear Creek, they were able to pack things away, get the fire safely doused, and be back on the trail within fifteen minutes. His belly full, Dog now darted back and forth into the areas to either side of their line of march, looking for things to chase.

As Caleb had predicted, it was approaching dusk when they reached the base of the foothills. The evening mist was already starting to form, and the sky overhead was a dusty blue with gauzy wisps of clouds like stray brush marks. The moon, high in the sky to the east, was like a big silver dollar as it reflected the light of the setting sun, which was behind the mountains to their west.

"Looks like the mist's gon' be heavy tonight," Caleb said. "I'd best get a fire goin' first, then I'll set up the tent."

"I will start putting up the tent," said Flora.

"You sure you can handle it by yourself?"

"You forget, husband. It is the women of the Shoshone who put the tepees up, while the men sit around the fire and brag about their hunting."

Laughing, he started looking for firewood. By the time he'd gathered enough and got the fire going good, Flora already had the tent up and was shaking out their sleeping gear.

"Dang, woman, you put that thing up faster'n I can do it."

"It is much easier than a tepee," she said. "Smaller and not so heavy. Now, finish shaking out these blankets while I get our supper started."

Caleb shook the dust and lint out of the blankets, folded them, and placed them side by side in the tent. He tested the tautness of the tent sides, and found that they were as tight as a drumhead. He was impressed. Most people threw a tent up and let it sag, so that when the wind blew it flapped and made noise, keeping the occupant or occupants awake all night. This tent wouldn't flap in anything short of a gale-force wind. He smiled and turned back toward the fire, where Flora knelt, looking at him with an enigmatic smile on her face.

"Nice job with the tent," he said. "Couldna done it better myself."

"I know that," she said simply. "Supper is ready."

Dog, who had been sniffing around the perimeter of their camp, came running and plopped down on his rear beside her, looking up with his tongue lolled out, and an expectant look on his face.

Caleb stopped next to him, an expectant expression on his face. He took in a deep breath. The aroma of beans and coffee warred with each other for his attention. His mouth watered, and his stomach gurgled. Flora laughed.

She put food in Dog's bowl and sat it down. He began eating noisily. She then filled a plate for Caleb and one for herself and sat on the extra blanket that Caleb had put there for her.

The two of them ate in silence, smiling down occasionally at Dog who made enough noise eating for the both of them. After their meals were finished, and the plates cleaned, Caleb poured two cups of coffee and they sat, shoulders touching, gazing into the fire.

Every now and then, they would gaze out beyond the fire, where the mist billowed and rolled over the ground like a living thing, so thick in places nothing could be seen behind it.

"Mist is pretty thick," he said. "Never seen it so thick this time of year."

Flora put her head on his shoulder.

"Many spirits are troubled," she said. "They live in the mist, and when they are troubled, they come out to ease their suffering."

Caleb wasn't much for superstitions, but he had to admit the thickness and constant movement of the mist as it circled around their camp site made him uneasy. He put his arm around her shoulder, and pulled her close.

"Well, I hope they get their troubles sorted out by mid-mornin'," he said. "We got lots of work to do."

4.

When they woke up the next morning, the mist still hung over them, but it was thinner, and not moving, so was less unsettling.

After stoking up the fire and getting the coffee going, Caleb went in search for more firewood. Flora had breakfast ready when he came back with an armload of wood. They ate in silence again, and after his second cup of coffee, he stood and dusted off his trousers.

"I think the mist's thin enough I can hunt," he said. "You might wanna wait 'till it's a mite thinner to go lookin' for your plants. I'll leave Dog here with you. He ain't no good at deer huntin' anyway."

"I can look for plants close around here. When the mist clears, I will look farther out. Dog can help me by scaring away the rabbits."

"Oh, he'll do that all right, 'n everything else that can move, too."

She was sitting by the fire, sipping coffee and petting Dog's head when Caleb, holding the rein of his pack horse rode into the mist surrounding the camp, and was soon lost from view.

"Well, Dog," she said. "I suppose it is just you and me now. Would you like to go hunting herbs with me?"

Dog made a 'whuff' sound and rested his muzzle in her lap.

"I suppose that means 'yes'," she said. She finished the last of the coffee. "Very well, let us go."

As if he'd understood what she said, Dog jumped up and ran ahead of her as she picked up her wicker basket and followed.

13

She decided to make a wide circle around the camp, staying close. The mist wasn't as thick as it had been when she and Caleb had crawled out of their tent, but was still thick enough to cause her to have to peer closely at the plants around her.

It didn't take long for her to find one of the plants she wanted. It's fuzzy, gray-green spiked leaves stood out from the darker green grass even in the mist. Mullen was used to treat swelling in the joints, and the tea was soothing and thought to help overcome the effects of colds in winter. It was also quite pleasant to drink the tea with honey instead of coffee on cold mornings.

There were ten plants growing in the shade of a pinyon pine tree, another of the plants she sought. She carefully plucked five leaves from each plant, leaving enough to allow it to continue to grow and flourish. Then, she gathered nuts from the lower branches of the pine. These were not for medicinal purposes, but was one of the main foods of her people when they'd roamed the hills and forests.

She smiled as she lifted her basket and resumed following Dog who was busy darting from bush to bush, sniffing and marking his new territory with streams of urine.

Her next discovery, ten minutes later, brought a broad smile to her face. White sage plants, with gray-green leaves like the mullen plant, but shiny, topped with tiny white flowers, had a variety of uses, from treating coughs, headaches, stomach aches, diarrhea, flu, and fevers, and more importantly for her, as a palliative during her monthly cycle. Again, she took only a few leaves from each plant.

Her basked was becoming heavy. She thought it might be a good time to go back to camp. She looked around for Dog, who stood, his tail up and his ears pinned back, growling at a stand of trees twenty yards from her.

"Come, Dog," she said. "We must get back to the camp."

For once, he failed to obey her. He continued to growl. A stab of worry and unease hit her in the pit of her stomach. Something was bothering Dog, and whatever it was, it had to be bad to cause the usually playful dog to act the way he was acting.

Slowly, she began walking toward him.

When she came to his side, and put a hand on his head, he relaxed a little, but continued to make rumbling sounds and stare at the gloomy shadows beneath the trees.

She could see a large, dark shape in the shadows, and the smell of blood assailed her nostrils.

Part of her mind was screaming at her to turn around and get back to the camp as fast as possible, but another drove her to move closer to investigate the strange shape. As she moved forward, Dog kept pace with her, his body rigid and his tail up.

Twenty-five feet from the shape, now seen as one large and three small shapes, the smell of blood was so strong she felt her stomach recoil. She fought to hold her breakfast down. A few feet more, and the mist began to dissipate enough for her to make out what she was seeing, and what she saw brought tears to her eyes.

A brown bear, its thick fur matted with coagulating blood, lay on its belly, its front legs splayed out in front, the long, razor-sharp claws black with dried blood. In front of the dead bear, their bodies mangled and broken, lay three wolves, their snouts, what was left of them, caked with dark stains.

Her mind quickly formed a picture of what had happened. The wolves, hungry and desperate, had attacked the bear, who had ravaged them with its claws, but they'd inflicted enough wounds to cause the bear to slowly bleed to death.

She whispered a prayer for the spirits of the dead animals to find peace in their afterlife, and was just about to turn away when Dog barked, and out of the corner of her eye, she spotted movement near the hindquarters of the big bear.

Afraid that the animal wasn't yet dead, she took a step backwards, her hands going to her mouth.

But the big bear, its eyes open but unseeing, was clearly dead. Looking more closely, she saw a brown bundle moving just inside the corpse's left rear leg, and heard a snuffling sound. Slowly, she approached, keeping an eye on the dead bear's mouth and dangerous front claws. As she drew even with the head, she saw that the bundle was a small cub, trying to push its snout under the belly of the dead bear.

"Oh, you poor thing," she said to the cub as it vainly sought a teat. "You're barely old enough to be weaned, and you have lost your mother."

The picture in her mind became clearer. The bear, a female, had been fighting the wolves who had in all likelihood been after the cub, smaller prey that they could have easily taken down. As any mother would, she had sacrificed her own life to save her young.

Flora knelt beside the cub and gently stroked its back, an action that it seemed to appreciate after trying in vain to get sustenance from the cooling bulk that had been its source of nourishment and comfort.

As she started to rise, the cub tried to follow her hand, but its legs wobbled, and it plopped down with legs splayed out.

"My goodness," she said. "You're weak from hunger, you poor thing." She looked at her basket. "I know, I'll find a rock and grind some pinyon nuts for you."

As she moved to the basket, the cub made the snuffing sound again, and then a mewling sound like a kitten crying for its mother. Dog, taking his cue from Flora's calmness, moved to the cub and sniffed it. Weakly, the young bear turned its head and sniffed back. Both animals seemed to decide at the same time that neither was a threat. Dog licked the cub, and sighed and lay down. Dog lay down beside it.

Flora smiled at the sight. She searched around until she found two stones, one flat, about six inches wide, and the other oblong, about the size of a peach. It wasn't her mortar and pestle, which had been left at camp with the other supplies, but she would make do.

She took two hands full of pinyon pine nuts and spread them on the flat rock, and then patiently ground them until they'd formed a moist paste. She then took the flat rock back and taking a small amount of the past in her hand, placed it near the animal's mouth. The cub sniffed, and then stuck out a long pink tongue and swiped the paste from her hand.

"You like that, do you? It's not your mother's milk, but it is good for you."

She continued feeding the cub until the paste was gone.

"Now, what am I to do about you? I cannot leave you here to die, but you cannot walk, and you are too heavy for me to carry."

She laid a finger against her nose and thought. Then, an idea hit her. She walked around until she found several slender branches that had not yet become dry and brittle. Using the tough reeds that grew all around, she fashioned a makeshift travois and with some effort, rolled the cub onto it. She slung her basket on her back, lifted the end of the travois, and began the long, arduous trek back to camp.

5.

She was bone-tired when she arrived at the camp site. Every muscle in her arms, back, and legs ached.

Caleb, with two deer carcasses slung over the back of the pack horse, came riding into camp from the opposite side.

"Hey, Flora," he said. "I had a good hunt as you can see. Bagged two young bucks. What you got there? Looks mighty heavy."

She was too tired to respond. She just let the end of the travois drop and pointed, looking at him.

He dismounted and rushed to her side.

"What the--! Is that what I think it is?"

She nodded, and began trying to remove the basket from her back. He quickly helped her, his eyes never leaving the burden on the travois.

"You wanna tell me where 'n how you come by . . . this?"

She put a hand on his arm for support, and began walking toward the now-dead fire.

After taking in a deep breath, she said, "Let me get a fire going so I can warm up, and I will tell you."

Caleb got the fire going and started a pot of coffee. Flora sat cross-legged and held her hands over the fire to warm them. As the circulation came back, her body relaxed, and she told Caleb about finding the cub.

"I saw a pack of wolves up where I found these deer," Caleb said. "Seem to be more wolves than usual for this time of year. Might be a good idea for you to stay close to the camp while I skin 'n dress them two deer. The smell's liable to draw 'em down here."

Flora hugged herself and shivered.

"I agree with you, husband. I think I can find what I need close by." She pointed at her basket. "I found many of the things I wanted this morning. I only need a few more, and I will have a good supply for the coming winter."

Caleb rubbed her shoulders.

"Good. Now, what we gon' do with our little friend over yonder?"

They looked in the direction of the cub. It had stood on the travois and was rubbing noses with Dog. The cub was still wobbly, but was able to follow teeteringly as Dog wandered toward the fire.

"We cannot leave it here to die, Caleb."

"Naw, I don' reckon we can do that. 'Sides, him 'n Dog seem to have developed a friendship. Okay, I'll rig up something he can ride in, 'n we'll take 'im home. But you know, he's gon' be gittin' too big pretty soon. You gon' have to let 'im go back to the wild where he belong."

"I know that, but until he is able to survive on his own, I will take care of him."

Dog and the cub sat near the fire, alternating their gazes from the flickering flames to the two large two-legged creatures seated next to them. Caleb smiled. This would be one strange bear, he thought. Most wild animals are spooked by fire, but, this one, like Dog, seemed to enjoy sitting near the warming fire. Dog yawned, making an 'owr-r-r' sound. The cub made a snuffling sound.

"Bear sure make a funny sound," Caleb said. "Ain't never heard it before."

Flora smiled at the cub.

"Caleb Johnson, you are not calling this little fellow 'Bear'. You have no imagination when it comes to naming animals."

Caleb shrugged.

"Well, if you ain't gon' call 'im Bear, what else you gon' call 'im?"

The cub made the snuffling noise again.

Flora smiled.

"I think I will call him Snuffy, because of the sound he makes."

Caleb rubbed at the bristle on his jaw.

"Snuffy? Hm, don' sound half bad."

Charles Ray

6.

Flora, with Dog and Snuffy for company, spent the next four days scouring the area around their camp, out to about a hundred yards, while Caleb skinned, gutted, and dressed the two deer. She found yarrow and sumac, and added to her store of pinyon nuts. In addition, she found more mullen in a grove of trees near the camp.

After finishing the deer, Caleb built a sturdier travois, to be pulled by Flora's pack horse. He scraped the deer hides and wrapped them back around the carcasses to go on his pack horse.

When they left the camp early one morning, the mist was just creeping in, tendrils of wispy white vapor snaking down the slope and wrapping itself around the trees.

They didn't make good time for the first two days. Cub, his energy buoyed by the ground pinyon nut mash Flora had been feeding him, often jumped off the travois to try and follow Dog as he darted around looking for rabbits to chase.

The return trip took them twice as long, but by the time they arrived back at their cabin, everyone was in good spirits. Snuffy had become a part of the family.

For the first three weeks, the cub was allowed to sleep in front of the stove snuggled up to Dog, but as his body began to fill out, and his natural nosiness caused him to smash furniture and overturn food containers, both Caleb and Flora realized that other sleeping arrangements would have to be made.

Caleb added a stall in the barn, and after some coaxing, mainly with pinyon nut mash mixed with sugar, convinced Snuffy that his new home was acceptable. That was made easier when Dog took to sleeping in the stall with him, or at the entrance. In fact, Caleb noticed that Dog and Snuffy were nearly inseparable. Where you saw one, you soon saw the other. Dog had taught Snuffy to chase rabbits, and the cub had taught Dog to rummage in containers for food. To Flora, it was both amusing and aggravating at the same time.

As Snuffy grew larger, though, Caleb was more concerned with what they were to do with him.

He would, Caleb, soon be too large for the stall, and the call of the wild would be summoning him. The problem, as Caleb saw it, though, was whether or not Snuffy, who had become accustomed to food being provided, to being rubbed and petted, and who had become the adopted brother of a dog, would be able to survive in the wild. Would other bears accept him? Would he be able to deal with wolves and other predators? Would he even know how to find food on his own, or worse, would he, after becoming accustomed to the food that Flora provided, even know what to look for.

The winter came and was replaced by spring, and Snuffy had in that time almost outgrown his stall. He and Dog now slept on a pile of straw in the center of the barn, and during the day, he and Dog followed either Caleb or Flora around like ducklings following their mother, sniffing everything, and trying to stick their snouts into everything.

March had been chilly, with the icy sting of winter lingering, and the winds from the north still rattling the cabin's windows at night. But April, with its gentler breezes and frequent rain showers, was, when the sun shone, much more to Caleb's liking.

It was also time, he decided when Snuffy, chasing Dog exuberantly around the yard, had crashed into the corral fence, smashing the bottom board, and scaring the heck out of the horses, who had only grudgingly accepted his presence in their vicinity.

Flora, who was hanging wash up to dry, stopped what she was doing and stared, mouth agape.

Caleb scowled.

"Flora," he said. "I reckon it's time we thought about sendin' Snuffy back where he b'longs."

Flora gave him a sad-eyed look.

"I know, but I will miss him. So will Dog."

"Shoot. Dog's got the attention span of a skeeter. He'll forgit about 'im two days after he's gone."

"But I won't."

Caleb shook his head.

"Me neither, but it's got to be done. He's gettin' just too big. 'Sides, it's 'bout time he learned to be a bear."

Flora walked to where Snuffy sat near the broken fence with a contrite expression. She put an arm over his shoulder and rubbed his ear. He made his characteristic snuffing sound and rubbed his head against her side.

"See," she said. "He's sorry for what he did."

Caleb walked over and squatted in front of the bear. He cupped its head in his big hands and spoke softly, "I know you didn't mean to break the fence, Snuffy, 'n I ain't mad at you," he said. "But I think it's time you learned how to be a proper bear. You can't do that livin' here in our barn. You gon' have to go back to the woods where bears b'long."

Snuffy made a low moaning sound, and licked Caleb's face with his raspy tongue.

Caleb stood and wiped his face.

"I'd best take 'im out 'n cut 'im loose right now," he said. "If I don't I ain't gon' be able to."

7.

Flora refused to accompany Caleb, Dog, and Snuffy when they left, heading west toward the foothills, afraid her emotions would show, making it difficult, if not impossible, to shoo Snuffy into the woods.

For his part, the bear treated it as another fun outing with two of his friends—his attitude toward the horses was much the same as theirs toward him, grudging acceptance of their presence, and not much else.

When they reached a point about ten miles from the cabin, where the thick forests began, Caleb stopped and dismounted.

He faced Snuffy.

"Okay, Snuffy," he said. "Time for you to go learn what bein' a bear's all about."

Snuffy pushed his head against Caleb's chest and made his snuffing sound, then whined, making a sound like the one Dog made when he wanted to go out in the middle of the night to do his business. Dog leaned against Caleb's leg, his head hung low, as if he knew this was a necessary thing to do, but, at the same time, not wanting to say goodbye to his friend.

Finally, Caleb pushed away from Snuffy.

"All right, bear. You got to git out in them woods 'n learn to be a bear. You can't stay in out house; you too dang big, 'n 'sides, people already lookin' at me funny every time I go to Bear Creek, 'cause they know I got a bear at my place. Jest a matter of time 'fore some skunk decides to take a shot at you."

Snuffy made a sound like, 'Rowr-r-r,' and stepped back from Caleb. For a moment, he looked as if wouldn't move. His head swayed from side to side. He sniffed the air, then let out a 'whoosh' of breath.

Bear and man locked gazes. Caleb would've sworn the animal was trying to communicate something to him, but danged if he knew what.

"Now, go on, Snuffy," he said gently. "You're gon' be all right. I know it." He pointed toward the trees.

Snuffy swiveled his head to look where Caleb was pointing.

"Go on. You know that's where you b'long."

Snuffy rose on his hind legs, as young as he still was, topping Caleb by a good three inches. He made his snuffing sound again, dropped to all fours, turned and began walking slowly toward the trees. He stopped every few steps and looked back as if expecting Caleb to call him back, but Caleb stood, silent and stone-faced, even though his stomach was churning, and his eyes stung from the unshed tears.

"Dang it," he muttered. "It's just a dang bear. I done kilt a dozen of 'em for their skins. How come I feel this way 'bout this 'un?"

He couldn't answer his own question. There was probably no sensible answer anyway.

After a few more trudging steps, and a couple more looks back, Snuffy picked up his pace, until, within fifty yards of the trees, he was loping along. He didn't look back anymore, and in minutes, he was gone, swallowed up by the shadows in the woods.

Caleb stood there for minutes, Dog at his side. Man and dog staring at the space in the trees into which their friend had disappeared.

Dog raised his head and howled.

"I know how you feel, Dog," Caleb said. "Kinda feel like howlin' myself. Oh well, ain't nothin' can be done 'bout it now. Let's go home."

He turned and walked to Horse and mounted. Without looking back, he nudged Horse toward home.

Dog took one last look at the woods in the distance, then turned and loped after him.

8.

Flora moped around the cabin for three weeks after Caleb took Snuffy away. She never complained, or said anything to him about it, but Caleb knew that, despite understanding the logic of what he'd done, she resented him for it a bit.

He decided he had to do something to pull her out of her doldrums.

One morning, a month after Snuffy's departure, as they were silently eating breakfast, he said,

"You wanna go into Bear Creek today? I hear Miz Stanhope got in some new material that'll make you a pretty dress for winter. Some kinda velvet stuff."

She looked up at him, a flicker of interest in her eyes.

"Really? Where did you hear that?"

"When I wuz out huntin' rabbits t'other day, I run into this fella from Bear Creek. He told me."

"I could use a new winter dress. Velvet you say?"

"That's what the fella said."

She nodded.

"Very well," she said. "We can go after I clean the dishes."

He helped her with that, and while she dressed, he went out and saddled their horses, and put a halter and long rein on his pack horse.

Her mood had brightened considerably by the time they entered the outskirts of Bear Creek, and by the time they entered Elvira Stanhope's shop, she was her usual smiling self.

"Good morning, Flora," Stanhope said as she turned at the sound of the bell over the door. "It's so nice seeing you today."

A short, slightly obese woman with snow-white hair and sparkling blue eyes, Stanhope waddled from behind the counter and embraced Flora.

"Good morning, Elvira," Flora said. "How have you been?"

"About as well as could be expected." She took Flora's hand and began pulling toward a counter upon which there were several rolls of fabric standing like fence posts. "Come, let me show you some of the new fabrics I just got in. I have a purple velvet that I think you'll love."

Both women were completely ignoring Caleb, something they had a tendency to do, so he left the shop, and went next door to Tom Stanhope's hardware store.

The bell over the hardware store's door was larger and louder than the dress shop. Tom Stanhope once told Caleb that it was like that because he was hard of hearing, and it was needed to let him know when a customer entered if he happened to be in the back of the store.

He was sitting on a stool behind the counter reading a newspaper when the bell clanged, announcing Caleb's entry.

He jumped off the stool and put the paper on the counter.

"Hey, Caleb, haven't seen you in a while. You looking for anything in particular today?"

Caleb shook his head.

"No, just brought the wife in so's she could do a little shoppin'. She been mopin' 'round the cabin for the last few weeks."

"Yeah? What had 'er down?"

Caleb told him about Snuffy. Stanhope looked at him with an expression of shock on his face.

"You had a bear . . . in your house?"

"When he started gittin' big, we put 'im in the barn," Caleb said. "But then eh even got too big for the barn, so I took 'im back to the wild. That's what got Flora all down in the mouth. She loved that bear, 'n danged if I don' think it thought of her as its mother."

Stanhope shook his head.

"I have heard of people around here doing some strange things, but that takes the cake. You, Caleb Johnson, are an interesting man, interesting indeed. Now, you ready to do some buying of your own? You know Elvira's going to be convincing that wife of yours to buy a load."

"Can't buy too much, Tom. We didn't bring but one pack horse."

"No worries. If you buy too much, I'll sell you a pannier real cheap."

"I jest might buy it anyway," Caleb said. "Always have a use for it. Lemme go look 'n see what you got interestin'."

Fifteen minutes later, he had a pile of odds and ends stacked on Stanhope's counter, a new pannier on the floor waiting to receive them, and was waiting for Stanhope to finish totaling up his bill.

"That comes to forty dollars," Stanhope said.

Caleb began counting out money from the leather pouch he wore around his waist. The bell over the door rang loudly, and a young boy came rushing in.

"Mr. Stanhope, Mr. Stanhope, ya gotta come quick, there's trouble over to y'er wife's store."

The boy came to a shuddering halt beside Caleb, breathing hard. He looked up at Caleb, and his eyes went wide.

"Y'er wife's in trouble too, Mr. Johnson," he said.

Caleb slapped his pouch closed, and whirled, running for the door. Stanhope, a shovel in his hand, grabbed from a large wooden barrel near the counter, was right behind him.

The two men crashed through the door of the dress shop, almost knocking the bell over the door off the frame.

Elvira Stanhope and Flora were in the corner in the back on the right, facing three men dressed in the clothing of ranch hands. Flora had the knife she always wore strapped around her waist in her hand, the blade forward.

"Now, squaw," a bowlegged man with dirty blond hair and a dull red scar on the right side of his face said. "Ya better put that pig sticker down 'fore ya hurt somebody."

"If you come any closer," Flora said. "I will not just hurt you. I will kill you."

The man laughed.

"Ya hear that fellas," he said. "This here squaw's got some grit, don't she?"

"Marvin Scarborough, you'd better get out of my store before I call the sheriff and have you and your scurvy friends thrown in jail," Elvira Stanhope said.

"Aw, shet your trap, ya old bag. This ain't got nothin' to do with ya. This is 'tween us 'n the redskin here."

Caleb felt a tightness in his chest and his cheeks burned.

"No, my friend," he said in an icy, measured tone. "This is between you 'n me."

The three men turned and saw a scowling Jacob, and an equally angry looking Tom Stanhope standing just inside the store. The scar-faced man, regarded them through narrow slits. The other two, a short, chubby man with dark, dandruff-flecked hair that covered his forehead down to his eyebrows, and a round-shouldered redhead with two upper front teeth that pushed out his upper lip. Looked surprised at their presence.

"This ain't your bidness, boy," scar face said. "This is 'tween me 'n the Injun here."

"Seein' as the *lady* you talkin' 'bout is my wife, it *is* my business, friend."

Caleb moved two steps forward, his fists clenched.

"That a fact? Done got y'erself a Injun woman, eh? Tell me, boy, how is it?"

Stanhope moved to stand next to Caleb.

"You're out of line, Scarborough," he said. "I think you should apologize to Mr. and Mrs. Johnson and then get out of my wife's store before things get ugly."

"Stay outta this, old man, this don't concern you."

"I beg to differ, sir. You're in my wife's store causing a ruckus, so that makes it of concern to me, now will you move, or do I have to go get the sheriff?"

Scarborough turned to the redhead.

"Buck Tooth, go close the door, 'n keep this old geezer outta my hair while I take this boy down so's I kin have me some sport with his squaw."

"Okay, Scarface," the bucktoothed one said. "But save some for me."

When he smiled, his prominent front teeth made him look like a redheaded rabbit. He circled around, looking at Caleb warily, and trotted to the door behind them. Caleb heard the snick of the lock and the scuffling sound of boots as the man behind them turned.

"Watch that hombre behind us," he whispered to Stanhope. "I'll take care of these two."

Stanhope nodded and turned to face the redhead.

"Okay, Billy Carson," he said. "You unlock that door right now, or I'll bash your head in with this shovel."

"Aw, c'mon, Mr. Stanhope," Carson said. "I don't wanna hurt ya. Whyn't ya put that shovel down."

Caleb had kept his attention focused on the two nearest the women. When the one called Scarborough reached for the knife handle sticking up out of his boot, he knew he had to move.

"Now, Tom," he said, and surged forward.

9.

Caleb was swinging his right fist as he moved, aiming at the Scarborough's chin. Not the best place to hit a man, but it was the best target at the moment, aided by the fact that Scarborough was leaning forward and not fully focused on Caleb.

His fist made contact just as Scarborough looked up. He felt the jolt all the way up his arm, and the stab of pain as his first two knuckles made contact with the hard bones of the man's jutting chin.

But it had the desired effect.

Scarborough's teeth clicked loudly, and his head snapped back. His eyes rolled back in their sockets and he dropped to his knees and pitched forward, his knife still in his boot.

The chubby one, standing with his mouth agape as his partner hit the floor, threw his hands up, palms out and waving, but too late, as Caleb was already swinging. His fist slammed against the man's temple, felling him like a tree.

Breathing hard, Caleb blew on the sore knuckles of his right hand, and turned to see Stanhope swing the shovel in a wide arc that landed against Carson's elbow as he put it up to block it.

"Ow," Carson cried. "You near broke my arm, old man."

Stanhope cocked the shovel for another swing, but Caleb caught his arm. He reached down and pulled his knife from the sheath attached to his lower leg and stepped up to Carson. He put the point of the knife against the man's Adam's apple and leaned in until their faces were only inches apart.

"Now, friend," he said in a hoarse voice. "Here's how it's gon' go. You gon' drag your two friends outta here, 'n when they wake up, you gon' talk 'em into gittin' on their horses 'n puttin' a lotta distance 'tween here 'n wherever you wanna go."

Carson swallowed hard.

"Scarface, uh, Marvin, he don't like bein' told what to do or where to go, mister."

"He like to be dead? 'Cause if y'all ain't outta my sight in the next few minutes, that's what he's gon' be, 'long with whoever happens to be runnin' with 'im. Do I make myself clear?"

"Yes, suh. Clear as rain water. Now, would ya take that Arkansas toothpick away from my gizzard, it's makin' me nervous."

Caleb pulled the knife back, but kept the point aimed at the man.

"Git to it, fella," he said.

Stanhope unlocked the door.

"While he's getting them out of here," he said. "I'm going to get a couple of shotguns just in case they wake up and want to start some more trouble."

Caleb nodded at him.

"Ain't a bad idea. They might decide to go by the sheriff's 'n git their own iron."

He watched as Stanhope trotted off, and Carson began to pull Scarborough by the shoulders toward the door.

"Could ya give me a hand?" he asked.

"Y'all didn't ask my help to start this ruckus," Caleb said. "You can stop it by yourself."

He crossed his arms and gave Carson a look that caused the man to shudder.

"Okay, okay, I'll do it myself," Carson said.

He'd dumped Scarborough outside and was pulling the chubby one out when Stanhope returned with two Remington single-barreled shotguns, and two boxes of shells. He handed a shotgun and box to Jacob. They followed Carson outside, where Scarborough was beginning to stir and make moaning sounds.

Carson dropped the shoulders of the man he was hauling, and knelt beside him.

"Dudley, wake up," he said.

The chubby man twitched, and opened one eye.

"That fella gone?" he asked quietly.

"What fella?"

"The one that banged me up side the head."

Carson glanced nervously over his shoulder at a glowering Caleb holding a shotgun across his chest.

"No, he's right here,' Carson whispered. "He got a shotgun too."

"H-help me up so I can git on my horse."

With Carson's help, the chubby man stood, swaying slightly when Carson released his hold on his shoulder. He blinked at Caleb, squinting at him through narrow slits. After gingerly touching the left side of his face which sported a large purple bruise just in front of his ear, and wincing in pain, he glared.

"Ya ain't had no call to hit me like ya did, fella," he said.

Caleb's expression, except for the tic of a muscle just under his left eye, didn't change.

"You lucky I didn't gut you like a fish. Next time you come near my wife, that's what I'm gon' do."

"C'mon, Scarface, let's git outta here. I done had my fill of this one-horse town," the chubby man said as he pulled himself up onto his horse.

Scarborough frowned at him.

"Aw, Dudley, ya gonna let this boy git away with what he done to us?"

"He wuz jest standin' up for 'is woman, Scarface. You'd of done the same if you wuz in 'is shoes."

"I don't like ridin' away 'n lettin' 'im git away with it, though."

"Well, that's what we're gonna do . . . for now. Let's ride."

Carson jumped on his own horse and followed as the two men, still bickering, rode down the street toward the sheriff's office.

"The fat one seems a reasonable fella," Caleb said.

"Don't you let Dudley Yates fool you," Stanhope said, shaking his head. "He's the most dangerous of the three. Scarborough is mostly mouth, and as you saw, Carson doesn't have much stomach for a fight. Yates, on the other hand, is just as likely to waylay you and shoot you in the back as to look at you."

Caleb looked at the three riders through narrow slits.

"I'll keep that in mind," Caleb said.

10.

When they went back inside the dress shop the two women were chatting away as if nothing had happened.

"You ladies okay?" Stanhope asked.

"Oh, yes," his wife answered brightly. "Those louts disrupted us just as I was showing Flora the new velvet fabric I got in, which was quite irritating, but other than that, we're fine."

"You could have been hurt." Stanhope's voice had a hurt tone.

"Hmph. Did you see that knife in Flora's hand? I do believe it would've been them that got hurt."

"That's a real possibility," said Caleb. "Flora's pretty good with that blade of hers."

She had returned the knife to its sheath.

"Flora, could you really cut a man?" Stanhope asked.

"If I had to," she said. "I was not about to allow those men to hurt my friend Elvira."

Stanhope turned to Caleb.

"Caleb, you got yourself a hand full here," he said. "Not so sure I'd want to get on her bad side."

Flora looked shocked.

"I would never hurt my husband," she said.

"Tom, stop teasin' these children like that," his wife said, wagging a finger at him.

"I think you 'n me better go back to your store," Caleb said. "Wouldn't want you gittin' in trouble with your missus."

"Yes, you should," the woman said. "I have to measure Flora for the frock I'm going to make for her."

The two men beat a hasty retreat.

Back in Stanhope's store, they finished the job of packing Caleb's purchases in the pannier.

"You'll like this," Stanhope said. "See these two leather straps at the top? If your load's not too heavy you can use them to carry it."

Caleb grasped the two straps and, bending his knees, lifted the pannier. It was a bit on the heavy side, but no more so than the usual load he put on his pack horse.

"You're right, it is handy," he said. "This is gon' make it a lot easier to git stuff we buy here in town back home."

"You know, Caleb, you should really consider buying a buggy or small wagon; maybe a buckboard."

"Now, why in blazes would I need that. That's jest one more thing I gotta worry 'bout fixin', 'n I'd prob'ly need another horse. Already got four, 'n dang if they don' keep me busy."

Stanhope shrugged.

"I sympathize with you, but when Flora buys a lot, especially fragile items, it's not easy to carry them on a pack horse. What if she buys a set of dishes and the like? Can you imagine trying to transport that on a pack horse without breaking half of them?"

Caleb shut his eyes and tried to imagine it, and the images that flooded his mind made him shudder.

"I'll think about it," he said. "Right now, though, we really don' need no wagon."

He took the loaded pannier outside, and lifted it onto his pack horse's back. The animal shied a bit at the strange load, but after Caleb patted its neck, it calmed down. He tied the cinches and adjusted the pannier to reduce any discomfort as much as possible. Satisfied that all was in order, he re-entered the dress shop.

Elvira Stanhope and Flora were still engaged in an animated conversation, which stopped when the ringing bell over the door announced Caleb's presence.

"Oh, Caleb," Flora said. "Wait until you see the cape Elvira is planning to make for me. It will be the most beautiful cape in the world."

"I'm sure it will," said Caleb. "Where's the stuff you bought. I'd like to put it in the pannier."

"The what?" Flora looked at him, her brows raised in a query.

"I bought a pannier to carry our stuff. We can fold stuff real nice. That way we don't have to get anything you bought all wrinkled on the trip home."

She smiled and inclined her head toward a pile of folded material that was half Caleb's height.

With a resigned look on his face, Caleb made two trips hauling her stuff out to the boardwalk. When he came out of the shop with the last bundle, he opened the pannier, and began stuffing it inside.

Flora grabbed his arm and pulled him gently away.

"My husband, you are sweet and generous," she said. "But you know nothing about packing delicate fabrics. I will do this."

Caleb stepped aside, and she proceeded to remove, refold, and repack everything, and even though he couldn't really see how she did it, everything fit neatly, was perfectly flat, and she'd even rearranged some of the things he'd bought from the hardware store. He smiled and shrugged.

"Looks like I don' know much about packin' anything," he said. "You got to teach me how you do that."

She patted his forearm.

"Living in a tepee, a Shoshone woman learns from the time she is a young girl to make everything fit into a small space. I am not sure it can be taught to one who has grown up among the white man where such things are not a problem."

Caleb wanted to tell her about some of the tiny settler cabins he'd seen, occupied sometimes by as many as six people, where they had to sleep two and three to a bed, but he didn't think she'd understand.

"Guess I'll have to let you do all the packing from now on."

"You would not have to learn if you would buy a wagon," she said.

His eyebrows did a little wiggle.

"Where'd you git that idea?"

"Elvira and I were talking," she said. "She thinks it would be easier for me to carry the things I buy if we had a wagon." She rubbed her round backside. "And, it would be more comfortable."

Dang, he thought, *now they're gangin' up on me. Ain't never had no wagon before, but looks like I'm gon' have one now.* "I'll give some thought to that," he said, knowing full well that he would buy a wagon, and the look on her face told him that she knew it too. "Now, let's git on home. I'm in a mood for some of your rabbit stew. That rabbit I kilt yesterday done smoked long enough."

11.

The very next week, Caleb did buy a wagon.

After thirty minutes of dickering with the owner of Bear Creek's largest livery stable, he settled on a buckboard, used but in good condition, that the livery station owner had recently put a new coat of dark green paint on. He paid fifteen dollars for the buckboard, and then spent another thirty minutes convincing Horse to allow himself to be hitched to it.

He found himself enjoying the ride back to the cabin. The metal springs under the buckboard's seat made for a smooth journey, without the jolting and pounding of his buttocks from Horse's gait. After a few minutes, even Horse seemed to be enjoying himself.

When he arrived back at the cabin, Flora was surprised and pleased.

"Caleb," she said. "You bought a wagon. What caused you to do that?"

The question was asked so innocently, Caleb thought at first that she was being serious. When he noticed the twinkle in her eyes, though, he knew that she was having him on.

"You know good 'n well what caused me to do it, woman," he said. "Now, what do you think? You gon' be okay with settin' atop this thing when we go into town?"

She clapped her hands.

"Oh, yes, my husband. I will be very happy." She rushed forward and embraced him as soon as he stepped down from the buckboard's bench.

"Now," he said. "You can wear dresses when you go to town."

She pulled back from him, eying him warily.

"You do not like when I wear pants?"

He waved his hands in protest.

"Naw, it ain't that," he said. "Hell fire, woman, you look right pretty in pants. It's jest that the other women in town is all wearin' dresses, 'n I thought you might want to be like them."

"Hmph. Why would I want to be like weak women who cannot go anywhere or do anything without their men?"

"You mean you don' like goin' places 'n doin' things with me?" Caleb had a hurt expression on his face.

She swatted his shoulder.

"You know that is not what I mean, Caleb. I love doing things with you, but I am also capable of doing things myself besides cooking, washing, and cleaning."

Caleb smiled. He grasped her shoulders and pulled her against his chest.

"I know that, Flora honey," he said. "That's what I love 'bout you. I wuz jest funnin'."

She snaked her arms around his waist and rested her head on his chest.

"It was not funny. If you wish for me to wear dresses like those weak white women, I will."

He kissed the top of her head.

"I wish for you to wear whatever you please 'n whatever pleases you. Now, do you want to go for a ride in your new buckboard?"

12

Flora took to driving the buckboard as if she'd been born to it. While it was originally constructed for a team of two horses, the livery station man had modified it to be drawn by one, and her horse, unlike Horse, did not object to being hitched up.

She would often take the buckboard out in her search for herbs and plants, and occasionally to hunt rabbits or other small game. Sometimes, when Caleb was busy working on hides in preparation for taking them into Bear Creek for sale, she would go alone, except for Dog who seemed to love trotting along beside the wagon. At others, the two of them would go together, with Horse tethered to the rear of the buckboard, and Dog still frolicking beside it. Even when Caleb went along, though, Flora insisted on driving. The only time he insisted on driving was whenever they went into town. He was an independent minded sort, but had no desire to endure the jibes that would come his way from the male population of Bear Creek if they should ever see him sitting meekly by while a woman drove.

Life settled into a comfortable routine.

Then, came that time of year when the breezes flowing down from the north were cooler, especially at night, the leaves of the hardwood trees began to become spotted with brown and orange, and they rose each morning to a mist creeping in from the foothills.

It was the time of year when life slowed down on the farms and ranches around Bear Creek. Farmers had harvested their crops and ranchers had pulled their herds in closer to their spreads. People were beginning to hunker down for winter.

Caleb and Flora, too, prepared for the winter, but unlike the farmers and ranchers, the pace of their lives picked up.

Caleb set out small iron traps for rabbits, and other small furry creatures whose fur grew especially thick when cold weather set in, making their pelts especially valuable on the fur market. Flora spent most of her time working in and around the cabin, occasionally venturing out a few miles seeking fall and winter herbs and roots which she used for both medication and food.

By mid-November, the cold had already settled in, and after one last trip to Bear Creek to stock up on canned and dry goods for the winter, Caleb and Flora stopped up any chinks in the cabin, stored up silage for the horses, and prepared to bunk in until spring thaw, with Caleb venturing out every three days to check his traps. Four times during the winter, he took his rifle and went hunting, each time bagging a rabbit, and on one occasion even bringing down four quails he caught foraging in the snow for food.

When they didn't have to go out during the day, he helped Flora prepare the meals, and they ate in silence. After meals, he would sit and read with her, or they would swap stories of their childhoods.

The one difference between this winter and the previous winters, something Caleb didn't notice until the frequent rains and early morning mist of spring started. The absence of wolves.

During previous winters he'd often found wolves had raided sprung traps, leaving nothing but the trapped hind leg of whatever smaller creature had been ensnared. This winter, though, not one trap had been disturbed, nor did he see one sign of a wolf pack on the prowl for prey. It was one of those things that wasn't in the forefront of his mind, but resided instead as a spark of curiosity in the deep recesses of his unconscious, emerging from time to time to nag at him. It was an anomaly, a divergence from the norm, and, except for changing his state from bachelor to husband, he wasn't fond of unexplained changes; he wasn't all that happy about changes that he could explain for that matter.

Winter changed slowly to spring, the first signs being green shoots sticking up through the melting snow, followed quickly by the spring mist. Unlike the autumn mist, which tended to glide in and hover over everything, the spring mist, stirred and roiled by the winds, was like a living thing. It never stopped moving, and caused things to appear to shimmer and shimmy as it enveloped them.

Where the mist that heralded the coming of winter was just mildly annoying, the mist that came at winter's end had a menacing quality about it that caused hunters and trappers to look over their shoulders every few steps, as if expecting something to spring at them out of the undulating mass of fluffy off-white clouds that hugged the ground and wrapped themselves around the trees and rocks.

Caleb had never been comfortable working in the mist. He hated not being able to see things clearly. But for reasons that he couldn't quite put his finger on, the mist this year bothered him even more than usual. When he went out in the mornings to retrieve his traps now that spring was approaching and animals would be bearing young, curious little creatures that he didn't want wandering into his traps, he felt a sensation between his shoulder blades like the touch of a warm poker pressing against his flesh. He glanced over his shoulder frequently, expecting to see something, but each time there was only the rolling mist.

No matter how he tried, he couldn't shake the feeling that he was being watched, that something or someone was stalking him.

One day, while eating lunch with Flora, he sat frowning into his coffee so intently, she looked at him with a worried expression.

"What is the matter, my husband?"

He told her of having the feeling that something in the mist was watching him when he was out retrieving his traps. After finishing, he sat there, staring into his coffee and feeling foolish. Finally, he shook himself and looked across the table at her.

"I know I'm jest bein' foolish," he said. "Ain't nothin' in that mist but mist. It's all in my mind."

"I would not be so sure, Caleb. Sometimes our minds tell us things that our eyes and ears do not see or hear. If you felt like you were being watched, you were probably being watched. Maybe the wolves have come back."

Welcoming anything that would help explain away what he viewed as crazy thinking, Caleb smiled at her.

"Yeah, you're prob'ly right," he said. "Wolves would be a bit spooky 'n stay back outta sight. Prob'ly sizin' me up to see if I was worth tryin' to pull down."

13.

By mid-morning the mist had cleared. The sky was a bright, icy blue, with a few fluffy clouds, and there wasn't much wind to speak of. The air still had a bit of a nip in it, just enough to cause Caleb to put on his deerskin jacket as he prepared to go out to retrieve the last of his traps.

Flora started pulling on her own deerskin jacket over her nankeen trousers and flannel shirt. On her feet she wore the deerskin boots that the Shoshone favored for cold weather.

"You goin' out to hunt for more roots 'n herbs?" he asked.

"I thought I would go with you," she replied. "We can take the wagon."

"Fine. I'll go hitch it up."

He jammed his hat down on his head and went out to the barn, followed by Dog, who immediately went to the corner of the corral and peed against the corner post. In the barn, the horses were pawing at the floor and snorting.

"Hungry are ya? Well, hang on 'n I'll git some grain for ya."

He scooped grain from a large bag in the corner and put generous amounts in each animal's trough, then watched as they ate noisily.

When he felt they'd eaten enough, he took his pack horse, the one he had been calling Mare, out and hitched her to the buckboard. Flora came out of the cabin carrying her wicker basket just as he finished. Dog followed close at her heels.

"Will one horse be enough if we happen to put a heavy load in the wagon?" she asked.

"Sure. This horse is used to carryin' a pretty heavy load. Pullin' a wagon ain't gon' be a problem."

He took her hand to help her up onto the buckboard seat. She slid over to the side with the brake, indicating that she would drive as usual. He shrugged and climbed up beside her.

"Where are we going first?" she asked.

He pointed. "Head west. See that sharp peak yonder? Keep that in front of you 'till I tell you to turn."

She whipped the reins, and Mare began walking forward.

"You can make 'er go a little faster," Caleb said.

"I do not want to tire her out before we have even put anything in the wagon," she said without looking at him. "Besides, there is no need to hurry. We have all day."

He had to admit, with the mist cleared, and no rain in sight for the moment, it was a pleasant day for a casual ride, and Dog was enjoying himself with time for many a foray into the brush along the trail.

Caleb sat back and put his arm on the top of the bench behind Flora's back, reaching up occasionally to massage the nape of her neck, which was now visible since she'd started wearing her hair up in the style favored by Elvira Stanhope. Only, on her it looked a thousand times better than it did on the portly shopkeeper. She leaned back into his hand and smiled.

Thirty minutes into the journey, he spotted the landmark he'd been looking for, a gnarled tree trunk that was all that was left of a towering tree that had been struck by lightning.

"Turn right here," he said. "Then we go north for 'bout five miles. Oughta be gittin' where we goin' by noon."

"Will that leave you enough time for what you have to do?"

He smiled and patted her back.

"More'n enough. I jest got three more traps to pick up. Heck, I'll have time for you to teach me how to recognize the herbs 'n plants you gather, so I can help you do that."

She smiled and leaned her head against his shoulder.

"That would be nice. Shoshone men do not do what they think is the work of women."

"Uh, I don' know then. If it's considered woman's work, maybe I ought not do it."

With her left hand, she slapped the top of his muscular thigh.

"That is foolish talk, my husband," she said. "You are more man than any warrior or hunter in my village. Only a true man can do things that women do and not feel less for doing it. Gathering herbs and roots can be hard work, and we appreciate when help is offered."

Her slap hadn't been an angry one, but it had stung. A testament to the strength in her hands, strength that had been developed by a life of back-breaking labor that was the lot of every Shoshone woman. They cooked the meals, erected the tepees, fetched the water and firewood, took care of the children they bore, while the men hunted, and on occasions fished, but fishing was for many of the men also considered work for women. He hadn't made definite plans for a trip to visit her people, but looked forward to the turmoil she would bring with all the new things she was learning and the new attitudes she was developing.

Oh yes, he thought, the next time Black Bear and Spring Flower visit will be a time that will be talked about around the council fires for generations. The thought made him smile.

Charles Ray

14.

They arrived at the area where he had traps to retrieve just before the sun reached its highest point.

"I'll fetch some wood for a fire," he said. "We can eat 'fore I pick up my traps."

She smiled and patted his arm.

"See, there is another thing that is considered woman's work among the Shoshone, yet you do it without thinking about it."

"Don' make no sense for that to be thought of as work for a woman," he said. "How in blazes do the hunters cook their food when they're away from the village?"

"Most of them take pemmican or pinyon nuts and eat them cold. Only the oldest and most experienced hunters bother making a fire. The ones who have learned not to be foolish."

"I ain't old yet," he said, smiling. "But I hope I ain't still foolish."

She laughed and slipped down from the buckboard before he could get off and help her down, and went to the back to unload their cooking gear. He hopped off and began to gather firewood, glancing her way every few minutes and smiling.

As soon as he had the fire going, she gently nudged him aside and began brewing a pot of coffee, heating some canned beans in a pan, and frying some strips of venison in a skillet. The combination of aromas caused Caleb's stomach to rumble, earning him a frown from her.

"The food will be ready soon, Caleb," she said. "It will not cook any faster if you stand and look over my shoulder. Would you go and see if you can find some more water? I noticed that two of the canteens are only half full."

Caleb knew when he was being dismissed like an annoying child. He huffed, but went to the wagon and took out the two lightest canteens. Opening them, he saw that she was right, though. The level of water was almost at the half-way mark. He poured water from one to the other, filling it, and headed toward a little spring he knew with the empty one.

The spring was in a clearing fifty yards from where they were camped. A small pool of crystal-clear water. Tracks of dozens of small animals dotted the soft ground around its edges. He even saw the hoof prints of deer. He made a mental note to come back to the spot in the fall when he did his hunting for winter meat.

After filling the canteen, he returned to camp, where a cup of hot coffee and a plate of pork, beans and biscuits awaited him.

When the meal was finished, he told Flora he would leave the buckboard with her and walk his trapline to retrieve his traps.

"You do not need to do that, Caleb," she said. "I will only look for plants nearby. You should take the wagon to carry the traps."

He patted her shoulder.

"Nah, I can handle it. Ain't that many, 'n they ain't that heavy. 'Sides, I need the walk to work off that fine meal you jest fed me."

She smiled and nodded her acceptance.

With his rifle on his shoulder, Caleb set out.

Although well camouflaged and invisible to the untrained eye, Caleb had no trouble locating his traps, all of which were empty. He carefully sprung each and slung it over his shoulder.

When he'd retrieved the final trap, he started back toward their camp. That was when he noticed that mist was beginning to form.

It struck him as unusual. The mist usually didn't start forming until just before nightfall. Yet, here it was in the early afternoon, already beginning to billow around the base of the trees and envelop the smaller bushes. For reasons that he couldn't fathom, it made him uneasy.

He quickened his pace.

Again, he had the feeling that he was being watched, which only added to his anxiety.

With each passing minute the mist thickened and his unease and sense of being watched grew.

When he got back to the buckboard, Flora was coming out of a stand of trees with Dog at her heels. When she saw the look of worry on Caleb's face, she hurried to his side.

"What is the matter, Caleb?"

He looked around. He saw nothing, heard nothing, but still could not shake the feeling of being watched.

"I don' know, Spring Flower," he said, using her Shoshone name in his anxiety. "I just have this itchy feelin' of bein' watched."

"Have you seen anything or heard anything?"

"No, not a thing, but I've learned to trust my gut on things like this. One time, when I wuz up in the middle range huntin' I got it, 'n ignored it. Almost got myself et by a grizzly. There's somethin' out there watchin', I just know it."

"Do you think it might be the wolves returning to their normal hunting grounds?"

"Could be." He looked down at Dog. "But I doubt it. If there wuz a wolf within half a mile, old Dog here 'ud have his hackles up like you wouldn't believe. No, it's somethin' else."

"But if it bothers you should it not also bother him?"

Caleb's eyebrows met in little arcs above his nose.

"You got a point. Maybe I'm just reactin' to bein' cooped up in the cabin all winter. You done huntin' roots 'n herbs?"

She held her basket up. It was filled to the brim with mushrooms.

"Yes. I found a nice crop of mushrooms in the trees there. They are nice when cooked in stew or with steak."

He took the basket from her and put it in the back of the buckboard along with the traps he'd had strung over his shoulder. There was also a wide assortment of herbs, roots, and other plants he didn't recognize.

"Look like you been busy," he said.

"Yes, the spring herbs are plenty, and I have picked enough to last until the fall."

"Good. Hop on 'n let's go. Dog, let's go home."

After hitching the horse up, he helped her up onto the bench and climbed up beside her. He flapped the rein and the buckboard began moving. He had to restrain himself from urging the horse into a trot. Now that they were leaving the area, the sense of being watched had lessened; not completely gone, but not quite as intense. He didn't want Flora to think he'd gone crazy.

"I know you are worried, Caleb," she said quietly.

"What tipped you off?" He smiled.

"You called me Spring Flower. That is the first time you have used my Shoshone name in a long time. That is how I know something is bothering you. I wish I could make the bad feeling go away."

"Oh, I think it'll go away once we git home. Maybe I'm just hungry for some of your cookin'."

She laughed, and that lifted his mood.

The mist near the cabin was beginning to thicken when they came within sight of the structure, softening and blurring its outlines from a distance.

"Looks like the fog's gon' be thick tonight," he said.

"I think it will rain," Flora said.

That was one possible explanation, certainly better than anything Caleb had come up with. Spring rains, though, were common. The mist was also common, but not as thick as it was. He wondered if it signaled a bad turn in the weather, which would interfere with his hunting and fishing. Maybe, he thought, that was what was giving him the uneasy feeling of being watched. He was not being watched, but was instead reacting to the strange weather.

That would be a sight better than really being watched. He smiled. It didn't seem to be bothering Flora—he winced when he remembered calling her Spring Flower, and that she'd picked up on it. She was much more sensitive to the wilds than he was, or so he felt. If she wasn't picking up strange feelings, it was all him.

Hell fire, maybe I am just hungry.

15.

Once the buckboard was unloaded and it and the horse put in the barn, Caleb went into the cabin where Flora had a hot cup of coffee waiting for him.

He sat at the table and cupped his hands around the container of hot liquid, staring morosely into it.

"Are you still worried about being watched from the mist, Caleb?" Flora asked.

He rubbed at his forehead.

"Kinda," he said. "But what really worries me is that you 'n Dog didn't git the same feelin'. Makes me think maybe I'm goin' 'round the bend."

She walked across the room and stood behind him, her hands resting lightly on his shoulders.

"I do not understand this 'going around the bend,' but if it means that you are not sane, I do not agree," she said. "If you feel that someone . . . or something was watching you, I believe you. Perhaps it was a spirit."

He looked up at her. Patting her left hand, he said, "I don' b'lieve in spirits, Flora. I know you do, but I been up in these mountains a long time, 'n whenever I felt somethin' was watchin' me, it was real."

"But why did Dog not sense it?"

"That's the part that's botherin' me. Maybe it's 'cause he wuz with you, 'n whatever was watchin' me was upwind of 'im."

She nodded.

"That would make sense. Did you feel like you were being watched when you came back to the buckboard?"

"No, not really. Just when I wuz up by the traps."

"Then, you are not crazy. Maybe it was wolves."

He smiled, feeling relieved that she didn't think he was going loco.

"You know, you prob'ly right. The wolves done come back, 'n they been hangin' 'round my traps hopin' they'd catch somethin'.'"

She walked back to the stove.

"Good. Now we can eat our meal in peace."

They ate in silence, occasionally glancing at each other across the table, and smiling. They were having cups of after-dinner coffee when Dog, who had been sleeping near the stove after filling his belly with scraps from Flora's plate, suddenly jumped up and ran to the door, barking furiously.

"What's wrong with you, Dog?" Caleb asked. "You smell a squirrel or a rabbit?"

Dog's ears were pinned back and the hairs on his neck bristled. He barked and scratched at the door.

"I do not think it is a small animal he smells," Flora said.

Her words were followed by 'pop' and the crash of broken glass as the front window to the left of the door shattered.

They both dove for the floor.

"Wha—"

Caleb was interrupted by a gruff voice from outside.

"Hey, boy, ya ready to die?"

16.

"Someone is shooting at us," Flora said. "Why? Who would do such a thing?"

"That voice sounds familiar. Sounds like one of the men who bothered you when you was at the dry goods store."

Tom Stanhope had warned him that the men who had harassed Flora and Elvira Stanhope were dangerous, but in the time that had passed, they had faded from Caleb's mind.

"Why are they shooting at us?" Flora asked. There was fear in her voice.

"I don' know."

He crawled across the floor until he reached the wall where his rifle hung. Standing slowly, he took it off the rack, and took a box of shells from the stand underneath the rack. He then dropped and crab-walked to the broken window. Easing up, he peered through the broken glass. The trees beyond their front yard were shrouded in swirling mist.

"Can you see anything?" Flora asked from where she lay on the floor.

"Nothin' but mist. I think they out there in that stand of trees, though." He stepped back from the opening in the window. "Hey, out there, why you shootin' at my house?"

"Ya didn't think ya could do what ya did to us 'n git away with it, did ya, boy?"

There was no doubt in Caleb's mind now. The voice belonged Dudley Yates, the fat man who had seemed reasonable, but who Stanhope said was the most dangerous of the three.

"I ain't done nothin' no other man woulda done," Caleb said. "Y'all ain't had no business messin' with my wife like you was doin'."

The man outside laughed harshly.

"Ya ain't seen nothin'," he said. "We're gonna have ourselves some fun with that squaw of yours, 'n ya gonna git to watch 'fore we put a bullet in your brain."

Caleb began to wonder if the uneasy feelings he'd had about being watched might be associated with the predicament they were now in. He found it hard to believe that the three ruffians would hold a grudge for so long. But that wasn't the big issue at the moment. He and Flora were trapped inside the cabin with only one way out, through the front door. Flora had on more than one occasion mentioned to him that a back door would be nice. It would enable her to get to the clothesline near the back of the house instead of having to haul dirty clothes out the front door and around the house. It would also have provided an alternate route of escape from just such situations as the one they were now in.

Not one to weep over spilt milk, though, he furiously thought of some way to solve the problem without there having to be any killing. Not one ordinarily to run from a fight, with Flora to consider, running was preferable to fighting if he was to keep her out of harm's way, and that was the thought that was uppermost on his mind.

He peered around the window frame, looking intently at the most likely place their attackers might be. He thought he saw a dark shape move within the mist. Bringing his rifle up, he snapped off a quick shot at the shape. He heard laughter.

"Jest keep shootin', boy," a voice called out. "When ya run outta bullets, we comin' in to git ya."

Caleb listened carefully, trying to locate the voice in the thick mist. He fired again, and was rewarded with a yelp.

"Dang, Scarface," a voice said. "He almost got me with that one. We orter move."

Caleb smiled. The second voice helped him focus more clearly on where they were. Of course, they would most likely move, but it would be to a position from which they wouldn't have such a clear and unobstructed line of sight on the front of the cabin.

"What will we do, Caleb?"

He looked down at Flora. There was a look of angry determination on her face, and she clutched her knife to her breast.

"First, we're gon' save our ammunition," he said. "They can't do nothin' but take pot shots. If they try to move in close, they'll have to come out in the open. They do that, 'n they're dead men."

A volley of rifle shots slammed into the walls of the cabin, but only one came through the window. Caleb felt the heat of the passing slug, and heard it hit the far wall. They were shooting blindly, most likely in an effort to entice him to shoot back and use up his ammunition. He wasn't' falling for it, though. He eased back from the window to avoid getting hit by flying shards of glass should a slug hit what was left of the glass in the window.

"We cannot stay here forever," she said.

"We can stay here longer'n they can stay out there. We got plenty of water in the barrel over there, 'n food enough to last for weeks. I'll bet they didn't think to bring food. When they git hungry, they'll either leave or do somethin' stupid."

More shots were fired. They sounded to Caleb like they came from different locations. Their attackers had split up, which would make it harder to pinpoint them. At the same time, though, if they tried to rush the cabin, they wouldn't be able to concentrate their fire. *Every coin's got two sides. Jest gotta take advantage of the good side of this.* He peered around the window, but all he could see was the dark shapes of the trees cloaked in the mist.

17.

Time seemed to stretch on into infinity. A soft breeze had come in from the north, but it did nothing to clear the mist, just caused it to whirl like low clouds in a windstorm.

While he'd been preoccupied with looking out the window, he hadn't noticed Flora stand and walk to his side. He became aware of her presence when he felt the warmth of her body touching his back.

"You should get back down 'n outta the way of fire," he said.

"I am tired of lying on the floor like a frightened child," she said. "If you fight, I fight."

He felt his heart swell with pride.

He handed her his Winchester.

"Here, take this, 'n I'll git my buffalo rifle. If you see anything move 'n it looks like a man, shoot it, but be careful 'n don' stay framed in the window too long. Don' want 'em to shoot you 'n ruin that pretty face."

She smiled and took the rifle. As he moved aside, she took his place at the window and began peering out for a few seconds, puling her head back, and peering again. He nodded in satisfaction and strode quickly across the room. He removed his buffalo rifle from the top hooks on the rifle rack, loaded it with shells from the table, pocketed ten extra cartridges, and went to the window on the left right side of the door. In order to have the protection of the thicker wall, he would have to shoot left-handed, something he hadn't done in a while, but now that he had his beautiful, brave wife fighting with him, he felt that he could do anything.

Even though it forced him to shoot off-handed, the position on that side of the door gave him a better view of the area in front of the cabin than the one on the left without having to stand in front of the window. He began to feel a bit more confident about their situation.

"If you ain't sure 'bout a target, don' shoot," he said. "Save your ammunition."

She nodded, put the Winchester to her shoulder, stepped back, and sticking just the first three inches of the rifle through the window, fired.

There was another yelp.

"Damn, I been hit," a whiny voice said.

Caleb recognized the voice of Bill Carson, the cowardly one of the trio of hooligans who had assaulted Flora. That meant that there was likely only the three of them, which in his mind made for odds that weren't as bad as he'd originally feared.

"Ya hurt bad?" Yates asked.

"It plowed a furrow 'cross muh arm," Carson answered. "It hurts like hell."

"Buck Tooth, ya ain't nothin' but a baby." The voice of the one called Scarface, Marvin Scarborough, dripped with derision. "Stop whinin', 'n shoot back dammit."

"Give the kid a break, Scarface," Yates said. "He ain't never been in a gun fight before."

Caleb smiled. They had drawn first blood, and already there was tension within the ranks of their attackers. If he could only take advantage of that somehow.

"Say Carson," he called out. "That's your name, right, Bill Carson? Why you let your friends talk you into doin' a foolish thing like this. They just gon' git you kilt. That ain't what real friends 'ud do."

"Doncha listen to that boy, Bill. He's jest tryin' to git under your skin."

"He done already got under it, Dudley. I got a furrow 'cross my upper arm, 'n it's bleedin' bad."

"I didn't do that, Carson," Caleb said. "That was my wife's shootin'. If it'd been me, I'd of put one through your head, but she b'lieves in givin' even skunks like y'all a chance to live."

"Ya lyin", boy," Yates said testily. "Ain't no woman can shoot like that."

Caleb raised the buffalo rifle and fired in the general direction of Yates' voice. At the same time, Flora fired the Winchester.

"That sound like a lie to you, Yates? How'd I shoot two rifles at the same time?"

He was answered by silence. He smiled.

Charles Ray

18.

The silence went on for a long time.

Caleb hoped, at first, that it meant Yates and his friends had pulled back. Then, a shot from the mist that passed through the broken window, mere inches from his face, disabused him of that hope.

"So, the squaw can shoot too," Yates said. "That's fine. I like me a woman with some fire in 'er gut."

Flora answered him by shooting in the direction of his voice. The sounds of muffled movement came from the mist.

"She got fire in more than her gut," Caleb called out. "If you ain't careful, she's gon' put some fire up your sorry backside."

For once, there was no sarcastic response. Caleb thought that Flora's shot must have come too close for the hooligan's comfort.

The next sound, though, surprised him. It was a piercing scream.

"Aiy-eee! Help! Git it off me. It's---" The scream for help was cut off.

"What is it Scarface?" Yates called. "What's the matter? Bill, go see what's wrong with that sumbitch."

"Okay, Dudley," Carson said.

A few seconds later, Carson yelled, "Oh, my Gawd! Oh shit?"

"What is it Bill?"

"He's all tore up. He's . . . oh, Lord, Dudley, hel—"

His voice too was cut off.

"What is happening?" Flora asked.

"Danged if I know," Caleb replied. "But whatever it is, it don' sound good."

"What the hell's goin' on, Bill?" Yates asked impatiently. "Will you 'n Scarface quit messin' 'round?"

More silence.

The silence bothered Caleb even more than the screams or being shot at for some reason. Something was going on out there in the mist, and he didn't know what. He hated not knowing.

Then, Yates screamed, a long, drawn-out wail of terror.

"Ai-i-iy-e-e-e-e-e-e-e—"

Again silence.

Caleb and Flora looked at each other. Her eyes were round, and she looked worried.

"What is happening out there?" she asked.

"I don' know," said Caleb.

He peered around the window, out into the gray mist. At first, the mist was all that he could see. Then, a large dark shape seemed to rise up in the mist, growing larger by the second.

Just as he raised his rifle to aim at the shape, Dog jumped up from where he'd been lying at Flora's feet and ran to face the door, barking and pawing at the wood. His barks were not those Caleb associated with anger or fear, but more the sounds he made when he wanted to go outside to romp around. That meant the shape, whatever it was, didn't trigger any canine alarms.

Flora looked at him curiously.

"He seems to want to go outside," she said.

"Yeah, 'n he don' seem worried." Caleb thought he must have imagined the shape in the mist. He looked outside again. The shape was still there, but was no longer moving. It seemed to be swaying from side to side, and he heard a grunting and snuffling noise. "Naw, it can't be," he said.

"What?" Flora now looked more puzzled than ever.

Caleb reached for the leather strap on the door.

"Okay, Dog," he said. "I'm puttin' all my trust in you."

Flora looked shocked and raised a hand.

"You are not opening the door, are you?"

Caleb nodded and pulled the door open just enough for Dog to squeeze through. The dog was out like a shot, barking and wagging his tail. Caleb went back to the window. Dog approached the shadowy figure without hesitation. The two figures merged in the mist, and he heard more of the snuffing sound.

"Well, I'll be doggone," he said. "Flora, you ain't gon' b'lieve who's out there."

"Who? What are you talking about?"

Caleb opened the door wide and stepped outside.

"C'mon out, 'n see for yourself." He started walking toward the two hazy shapes, one large and one small, that seemed to be touching.

He heard Flora's hesitant footsteps behind him.

As Caleb neared, the two shapes began moving toward him.

"Caleb, look out, it is coming toward you."

He didn't stop, and neither did the shapes. At about fifteen feet, they became clearer, and he smiled broadly.

"Hey, Snuffy," he said to the big brown bear that was rubbing noses with Dog. "Ain't seen you in a while. You done got mighty big since you went into the hills."

The bear looked up at him and opened its mouth wide, revealing rows of razor-sharp teeth.

It made the snuffling sound and then a kind of coughing that almost sounded like Dog. Dog barked and pawed at its hide. Snuffy inched forward until his nose was even with Caleb's face. He pushed his big black nose gently against Caleb's chest and snuffed, his plea for Caleb to scratch his neck and back.

When Flora, who had started running with her rifle raised when the big shape neared Caleb, saw what was happening, she stopped in her tracks.

"Snuffy. You have come back," she said.

The bear, upon hearing her voice, moved away from Caleb and shuffled toward her. When he reached her, he lay down and rolled over onto his back with his legs in the air. Caleb couldn't suppress a laugh. When Snuffy was a cub, he'd loved having Flora rub his stomach as much as Dog did, and would often interrupt her at work to get a belly massage.

Laughing, Flora rubbed with her left hand while keeping the rifle ready with the other.

Caleb understood her caution, but when Snuffy put his legs in the air, he'd seen the streaks of blood and bits of flesh and hair on the claws of his forefeet. The men who had been attacking him were no longer a threat. He wondered, though, if they were still alive.

A brown bear can grow to a height at the shoulders of five to eight feet, and a weight of 700 pounds, and Snuffy looked as if he'd made it near the top of the scale. He didn't look like he'd lost much weight during winter hibernation either. While brown bears eat mostly nuts, berries, fruits, leaves, and roots, they sometimes take down other animals, from small rodents to large bull moose. With claws two or more inches long and a running speed of thirty miles per hour, they can outrun a man and maul him horribly. Not normally threatening to humans, they will attack if threatened, cornered, or if something gets between them and their young.

Suddenly, Caleb understood why he'd been feeling that he was being watched. Snuffy had been watching him when he was retrieving his traps. Why the animal hadn't made his presence known, he didn't know, but it explained somewhat why Dog hadn't sounded the alarm. He hadn't smelled anything dangerous, and had probably associated Snuffy's odor with him and Flora.

He had a feeling he'd find what was left of their attackers somewhere out there in the trees, but decided that he'd wait until the mist cleared, and hope they didn't attract scavengers in the meantime.

"If y'all finished with the reunion," he said. "Whyn't we all go back to the cabin 'n git some grub."

"What about the men who were shooting at us?"

Caleb pointed to Snuffy's bloody paws.

"I got a feelin' they ain't gon' be bothering us no more," he said.

Charles Ray

19.

Too big for the cabin when Caleb had turned him loose in the hills, Snuffy was not too big to fit through the door. So, Flora brought him some honey-flavored mash in a bowl and fed it to him in front of the structure. After Dog whined and stared open-mouthed at her, she got some strips of meat and put them in a bowl for him. The two animals ate contentedly side by side as they'd often done with Snuffy was a cub.

Caleb took advantage of the calm to check on the other animals. The horses were still agitated from the shooting, and the smell of dried blood that the breeze carried from Snuffy's body to the barn. He quietened them down by putting fresh oats into their feed troughs and talking quietly to them.

While Snuffy and Dog romped around the yard, Flora went inside and cooked lunch. Caleb took two chairs outside and they brought their food out and ate while they watched bear and dog playing in the grass like two puppies.

"I think Dog has missed his playmate," Flora said.

Caleb nodded.

"I still can't b'lieve how them two git along."

"Snuffy has known Dog since he was just a cub. I think he sees Dog as just a strange, small bear, or maybe thinks of himself as a really large dog."

As if to illustrate her point, Snuffy again made the sound like a rough, raspy bark.

"Dang, I think you're right. 'Course, we got a problem now," he said. "He's too big to stay 'round here. Somebody see 'im, they likely to shoot 'im for that pelt of his."

Flora's forehead creased in concern.

"What will we do?"

"I don' know. I'll think of somethin'."

The mist had begun to clear at noon, and two hours later had almost disappeared except for a few clouds hovering over damp grass in places.

Caleb stood and stretched.

"Guess I better go find what's left of them fellas, 'n take 'em back to town."

She nodded at him, but kept petting Snuffy. He walked to the barn and took the pack horse, Mare, from her stall. He led her outside and tied her rein to a corral post, and then went back inside the barn and rolled the buckboard out.

He went back inside the barn and got several burlap bags, which he spread over the cargo area of the buckboard.

After he'd hitched her to the buckboard, he climbed up on the seat and picked up and flapped the reins, pulling Mare to aim her toward where he'd last heard voices.

Flora waved to him as he drove past. Snuffy and Dog, now both being rubbed by her, paid him no attention.

He found the first body about a hundred yards from the cabin.

20.

Marvin 'Scarface' Scarborough had been laid open from his left shoulder almost to his right hip. Long, evenly spaced gashes that had exposed ribs.

If he hadn't been killed outright by the force of the attack, Caleb thought, he didn't last long. The dark, still damp stain on the ground indicated a massive loss of blood, and the man would have bled out in seconds.

Caleb got down from the buckboard and, taking the corpse by the shoulders, heaved it onto the buckboard. He had to hold his breath against the stench coming from the already bloating body.

He found Carson next. His belly had been ripped open and intestines hung out like large ropes. His face was untouched, and his unseeing eyes were wide with the terror of the last moments of his life. His body was placed next to Scarborough's.

Dudley Yates' body was harder to find. After being attacked by Snuffy, Yates had crawled into the high grass, vainly seeking the shelter of the trees. Caleb found him with his back against a tree, covered in blood from chest to groin, his clothing in tatters. Surprisingly, he was still breathing, but Caleb could tell from the amount of blood pooled on the earth around him that he didn't have long.

Caleb doubted that the man could see him clearly, despite his eyes being opened. They were already clouding over. Under ordinary circumstances, and with almost anyone else, he would've tried to administer some kind of aid or comfort. This man, though, had tried to kill him and his wife. In Caleb's mind, he was no better than a rabid coyote who needed to be put down. He would've liked nothing better than to have been the one to do it, but Snuffy had beaten him to the punch.

He stood there, looking down without emotion as the final light fled from Yates' eyes, and with a last gust of breath that sent a stream of blood from between his lips, he gave up the ghost. His head dropped forward, and his body seemed to shrink as the last air left his lungs. Caleb waited a few more minutes, then moved forward, grabbed Yates' collar, and drug his body to the buckboard.

With the three dead attackers lying side-by-side in the buckboard, he drove back to the cabin.

He stopped the buckboard at the edge of the yard and got down. Flora stopped petting Snuffy and stood. As she walked toward him, he raised his hand for her to stop.

"You don' wanna see this," he said. "It ain't pretty a'tall."

She kept walking.

"I want to make sure for myself that they are dead," she said simply as she walked past him.

At the back of the buckboard, she stared woodenly at the three bodies. After a few minutes, she turned and walked past him back to the front of the cabin, where she resumed playing with the big brown bear who was rolling on the ground with Dog like a puppy.

"I'm takin' 'em to the undertaker," he said. "You gon' be okay here alone for a few hours?"

She smiled up at him.

"I have Snuffy and Dog to keep me company, and keep me safe," she said.

Caleb got back onto the buckboard and got the horse moving in the direction of Bear Creek.

Charles Ray

21.

When Caleb stopped the buckboard with its grisly cargo in front of the undertaker's, a crowd of people gathered immediately, gawking and pointing.

"What the devil happened to them?" asked the undertaker, a cadaverous-looking man with a widow's peak and hawk nose.

"Looks like they run into a grizzly," Caleb said. "Found 'em in the woods not far from my cabin."

The Bear Creek sheriff, a lanky man with flowing white hair and a white-streaked handlebar mustache, walked to the back of the buckboard and immediately recoiled, from the sight of the mangled corpses and the smell.

"Jumpin' Jehoshaphat, ya tellin' me *one* bear did this to three men?"

Caleb shrugged.

"I only saw one set of tracks," he said. "They wudn't all in one place. I reckon, they got spooked 'n started runnin' off in different directions. Ain't a good idea to run when you done spooked a bear."

The sheriff nodded.

"That's for sure." The sheriff turned to the undertaker. "Reckon ya got your job cut out for ya on this 'un. Ain't gonna be easy to fix these hombres up for viewin'."

"I seriously doubt anyone will want to view them," said Tom Stanhope, who had just come across the street from his hardware store. "This is Dudley Yates and his crew. They've been nothing but trouble for this town since they day they ended up here. I doubt anyone will even come to a funeral for them except to make sure they're dead."

The sheriff tugged at his mustache.

"Ya got a point there. Well, since they ain't got no family, I reckon ya jest have to stuff 'em in coffins 'n we'll plant 'em out at Boot Hill. I wonder what the hell they were doin' out by your place, Caleb. Most folks 'round here know not to hunt near your spread."

"I have no idea, sheriff," Caleb said. "Whatever it was, reckon they takin' it to their graves."

"It was neighborly of ya to bring 'em in."

Caleb smiled.

"I wudn't exactly bein' neighborly, sheriff. Can't have bodies stinkin' up my place 'n attractin' scavengers."

The sheriff laughed.

"They ain't gonna be stinkin' up nothin' but hell from now own." He turned to go, then stopped and turned back to Caleb. "I s'pose I'm still gonna have to do a report of this for the county. Ya mine stoppin' by my office 'fore ya leave town 'n givin' me all the details."

"I surely will, sheriff."

Stanhope stepped up beside Caleb, and the two men watched the sheriff walk back to his office. The undertaker called his assistant out, and the two of them began hauling the bodies into the building.

Stanhope sniffed the air.

"It'll be a while before you get the stench out of your buckboard, Caleb."

"Yeah. Reckon Flora ain't gon' wanna be drivin' it for a while."

When they were finally alone on the boardwalk, Stanhope leaned in close to Caleb.

"That bear of yours come back, did he?"

Caleb looked around carefully, then said, "I don' think he ever really left."

"What do you mean?"

"Well, me 'n Flora wuz out. She wuz gathering roots, 'n I wuz pickin' up my traps. I kept havin' this feelin' of bein' watched, but my dog didn't seem to be bothered by anything. Then, these three showed up at the cabin, 'n started shootin' it up. By the way, this is jest 'tween me 'n you. Anyway, they wuz shootin' the place up. Then, we heard screamin', 'n when it stopped, old Snuffy come walkin' outta the mist as big as life. I think, 'cept when he wuz hibernatin' this winter, he's been watchin' over us."

Stanhope's expression was skeptical.

"A bear protecting people? That sounds crazy to me."

"If I hadna seen it with my own eyes, it'd sound crazy to me, too," Caleb said. "But we raised that bear from a little cub after his mama was killed by wolves. I think he sees himself as a big dog. After all, he growed up playin' with Dog. Hell fire, he likes nothin' better'n layin' on his back 'n lettin' Flora scratch his belly."

Stanhope laughed so hard tears flowed down his rosy cheeks.

"Now, that is something I'd pay to see," he said. "You could charge money for people to come see that."

"Wouldn't be a good idea." Caleb shook his head. "First off, you know how people 'round feel 'bout bears. Somebody's likely to try 'n shoot 'im for his fur, 'n second, if I did that, Flora 'ud kill me."

"Yeah, you don't want to cross that wife of yours, that's for sure. I'll bet when those ruffians started shooting at you, she shot back, right?"

"You know it. 'N when I brought their bodies back from the woods, she walked up big as brass to git a look to make sure they wuz dead."

Stanhope's expression turned serious.

"Are you planning to tell the sheriff what really happened, I mean, about them attacking your house?"

"Naw, I think it best to leave that alone," Caleb said. "They dead now, so ain't nothin' the sheriff can do 'bout it. I'm gon' jest let it go to the grave with 'em."

"I suppose you're right. If you told him, the sheriff would have to open an investigation, and that could take weeks. And, of course, there'd likely be some suspicion because of your previous encounter with them."

"Yeah, that's the other reason I don' plan on sayin' anythin' to the sheriff. They attacked us, but the way they wuz kilt, the sheriff might not b'lieve it."

Stanhope rubbed his chin and nodded.

"Well, Caleb, I'd better get back to the store 'n let you get your meeting with the sheriff over with. Give my regards to your wife."

Stanhope turned and walked away.

Caleb watched until he entered his store, then turned and started walking toward the sheriff's office.

"Might's well git this over with," he mumbled. "I hope Flora cooks somethin' real special for supper tonight."

BOOKS BY THIS AUTHOR

The Adventures of Deputy U.S. Marshal Bass Reeves

Fatal Encounter
The Marshal and the Madam
The Shaman's Curse
Renegade Roundup
Ma Barker's Boys
The Adventures of Bass Reeves, Deputy US Marshal (box set)
Bass and the Preacher
A Bad Day to Die
The Red River Queen
The Pinkerton
The Long Arm of the Law
The Penny Dreadful Writer
The Trial

Al Pennyback mysteries

Color Me Dead
Memorial to the Dead
Deadline
Dead, White, and Blue
A Good Day to Day
The Day the Music Died
Die, Sinner
Deadly Emotions
Death by Design
Till Death Do Us part
Deadly Dose
Dead Man's Cove
Dead Men Don't Answer
Deadly Paradise
Kiss of Death
Death in White Satin
Death and Taxis
Deadbeat
A Deadly Wind Blows
Death Wish
Deadly Vendetta
A Time to Kill, A Time to Die
Dead Ringer

Death of Innocence
Dead Reckoning
Murder on the Menu
Over My Dead Body
Bad Girls Don't Die
A Deal to Die For
The Dead Blonde in the Red Bikini
Return to Dead Man's Cove

Ed Lazenby mysteries

Butterfly Effect
Coriolis Effect
The Cat in the Hatbox
Negative Side Effects
Murder is as Easy as ABC
Body of Evidence
Who Killed Henry Hawkins?
Skeleton in the Closet

Daniel's Journey

Wagons West: Daniel's Journey
Wagons West: Trinity
Wagons West: Bounty Hunter

Buffalo Soldier

Trial by Fire
Homecoming
Incident at Cactus Junction
Peacekeepers
Renegade
Escort Duty
Battle at Dead Man's Gulch
Yosemite
Comanchero
Range War
Mob Justice
Chasing Ghosts
The Piano
Family Feud
The Lost Expedition
The Iron Horse

Park Patrol

Jacob Blade: Vigilante

Avenging Angel
Vengeance is Mine
Hot Lead, Cold Steel
The Vigilante From Texas
Hell in the High Country
Last State to Mesa Grande
Shootout at Heartbreak Ridge
A Fine Day for Dying
Vigilante League
Last Man Standing
Bullet from the Vigilante
The Guns of Jacob Blade
Vigilante Killer on the Run
Cold Steel
Heartbreak Ridge Shootout
The Last Stage Heading to Mesa Grande
The Last Gunfighter Standing
Sins of the Father
The Guns of Jacob Blade Vigilante
Vigilante Killer on the Run

Caleb Wolf: Bounty Hunter

Date with Death
The Missing Mail Order Bride
The Saga of One-Eyed Jack

Other Fiction

Angel on His Shoulder
She's No Angel
Child of the Flame
Pip's Revenge
Wallace in Underland
Further Adventures of Wallace in Underland
Dead Letter and Other Tales
The White Dragons
The Dragon's Lair

Dragon Slayer
The Last Gunfighters
The Culling
Frontier Justice: Bass Reeves, Deputy U.S. Marshal
Angel on His Shoulder – Revised Edition
Battle at the Galactic Junkyard
Mountain Man
Devil's Lake
Vixen
Awakening
Chase the Sun
The Lady's Last Song
Purgatory is the Next Stop
Dead Letter and Other Tales – Revised Edition
Catch Me if You Can
A Cowboy's Christmas Carol
Texas Ranger J.D. Pettit: Waxahachie War
Hard Ride to Glenrose, Texas
Toby Giles: Tarnished Badge
Tom Steele: Into Dark Lands
Marshals of Dusty Saddle (short story anthology)
Sheriff B.J. Kincaid: Shoot Fast or Die
Tom Steele: Demons at Dawn
Guns Along Carson's Ford (with Fred Staff)
Sheriff B.J. Kincaid: Cry of the Raven
Texas Ranger J.D. Pettit, Gunplay in Garrison
Breath of the Dragon
Sheriff B.J. Kincaid: Bullet for a Bad Man
Texas Ranger J.D. Pettit: Sweet Home, Sweetwater
Toby Giles: The Walls of Jericho
Tom Steele: A Day of Reckoning
Sheriff B.J. Kincaid: Showdown at High Noon
The Blazing Guns of the Lawman Kincaid
Texas Ranger J.D. Pettit: When the Cajun Came to Center
Toby Giles: One More River to Cross
Back to Bear Creek
The Calico Cowboy
Rendezvous at Red Rock Canyon
Menace in the Mountain Mist

Nonfiction

Things I Learned from My Grandmother About Leadership and Life
Taking Charge: Effective Leadership for the Twenty-First Century
Grab the Brass Ring
African Places
A Portrait of Africa
There's Always a Plan B
In the Line of Fire
Advice for the Insecure Writer
Looking at Life Through My Lens
Ethical Dilemmas and the Practice of Diplomacy
Making America Grate Again
DC Street Art
Things I Learned from My Grandmother, Second Edition
Feathers, Fur, and Flowers
Backyards and Byways
American Heroes
Invasion of the Swamp Creatures
Ethical Diplomacy and the Trump Administration

Children's Books

The Yak and the Yeti
Samantha and the Bully
Molly Learns to Share
Where is Teddy?
Catie and Mister Hop-Hop
Tommy Learns to Count
Catie Goes to School

Writing as Ben Carter

William Coburn: Cowboy vs the Sea Monster

Charles Ray

ABOUT THE AUTHOR

Charles Ray began writing fiction in his early teens, when he won a national Sunday school magazine short story competition, but, having been taught to read by his mother when he was four, and having read every gook in his school library by the time he reached fifth grade, he's been making up stories much longer. Painfully shy until mid-way through his freshman year in high school, writing was his primary form of communication—when he chose to communicate, preferring the company of books to people.

He joined the army in 1962, right out of high school, and during the next twenty years, along with soldiering, he moonlighted as a newspaper or magazine journalist, artist, and photographer in the U.S., and abroad. In the 1970s, he was the editorial cartoonist for the Spring Lake (NC) News, a small weekly, and did cartoons and art for a number of publications, including Ebony, Essence, Eagle and Swan and Buffalo (a now-defunct magazine that was dedicated to showcasing the contributions of African-Americans to American military history.

He retired from the army in 1982 and joined the U.S. Foreign Service, serving until he retired in 2012 as a diplomat in posts in Asia and Africa.

He's worked and traveled throughout the world (Antarctica is the only continent he's never visited), and now, as a full-time bohemian (a catch word for someone who engages in creative pursuits of all kinds), he continues to roam the globe looking for subjects to write about, photograph, or paint.

A native of East Texas, he now calls suburban Montgomery County, Maryland home.

For more information on his works, and other projects, check out one of the following sites:

http://charlesray-author.com/
http://charlesaray.blogspot.com
http://charlieray45.wordpress.com
http://www.twitter.com/charlieray45
http://www.flickr.com'charlesray45
http://www.viewbug.com/member/charlesray
https://fineartamerica.com/profiles/2-charles-ray.html

Authors write to be read, and that can only happen when readers are made aware of what they've written. Reviews are a great way to inform readers of new works, so if you've liked this book, please be so kind as to leave a short review on Amazon, Goodreads, or the site from which you purchased it.

Made in the USA
Las Vegas, NV
21 January 2021